Wishes and Wings

Read all the books in the
Faeries' Promise series:

Silence and Stone

Following Magic

The Faeries' Promise

Wishes and Wings

BY KATHLEEN DUEY

Illustrated by
SANDARA TANG

Aladdin
New York   London   Toronto   Sydney

With love and thanks to Ellen Krieger, my editor and friend, for publishing my first book and so many more

ALADDIN
An imprint of Simon & Schuster Children's Publishing Division
1230 Avenue of the Americas, New York, NY 10020
First Aladdin hardcover edition March 2011
Text copyright © 2011 by Kathleen Duey
Illustrations copyright © 2011 by Sandara Tang
All rights reserved, including the right of reproduction in whole or in part in any form.
ALADDIN is a trademark of Simon & Schuster, Inc., and related logo is a registered trademark of Simon & Schuster, Inc.
For information about special discounts for bulk purchases please contact Simon & Schuster Special Sales at 1-866-506-1949 or business@simonandschuster.com.
The Simon & Schuster Speakers Bureau can bring authors to your live event. For more information or to book an event contact the Simon & Schuster Speakers Bureau at 1-866-248-3049 or visit our website at www.simonspeakers.com.
Designed by Lisa Vega
The text of this book was set in Adobe Garamond.
The illustrations for this book were rendered digitally.
Manufactured in the United States of America 0211 FFG
2 4 6 8 10 9 7 5 3 1
Library of Congress Cataloging-in-Publication Data
Duey, Kathleen.
Wishes and wings / by Kathleen Duey ; illustrated by Sandara Tang. —1st Aladdin hardcover ed.
p. cm. — (The faeries' promise ; [#3])
Summary: The human and faerie worlds intersect as the faeries return to their meadow home near Lord Dunraven's castle.
ISBN 978-1-4169-8460-3
[1. Fairies—Fiction. 2. Magic—Fiction.] I. Tang, Sandara, ill. II. Title.
PZ7.D8694Wk 2011
[Fic]—dc22
2010001080
ISBN 978-1-4424-1302-3 (eBook)

lida is a faerie princess. Gavin is a human boy. He helped her escape from Lord Dunraven's castle—and she saved his life. They are good friends, but old Lord Dunraven made a law sixty years ago that forbids magical creatures to have any contact with human beings. Alida's family moved far from the village of Ash Grove into the deep woods. They tried to obey that law. But now they have decided to go home. . . .

Chapter

1

It was a chilly morning.

The faeries were lining up, getting ready to leave. Everyone was busy. Gavin was helping carry crates of food.

Alida was scared and excited all at once. It was wonderful to be back with her family after all the years she had spent alone, locked away in Lord Dunraven's castle.

It had eased her heart to finally tell her parents about the silent little room in the stone tower and about her friendship with Gavin. She told them how he had risked his life to help her escape—and that she had freed him from Lord Dunraven's prison.

Her father said he was proud of her. Her mother hugged her and told her she was brave.

But Alida didn't feel brave.

Not now.

Her mother had decided it was time for them to return to the meadow near the human town of Ash Grove—which meant they would be breaking old Lord Dunraven's law.

Sooner or later his great-grandson would find out. Alida was so afraid he would send his guards to find her.

The thought of even *seeing* the guards again scared her breathless. The idea of being taken back to Dunraven's castle terrified her.

Alida glanced at her mother.

She was walking fast, checking things, making sure the faeries were lining up, getting ready to begin the journey home.

Alida was glad her mother would be leading the way. She had planned everything.

She had insisted that all the faeries wear clothing the color of oak leaves and grass and evening sky— so they would be harder to see in the forest shadows. She had even asked the weavers to make a brown shirt for Gavin.

It was still easy to spot him near the end of the line, though surrounded by her aunts and uncles. Eleven-year-old human boys were taller than faeries, even the grown-ups.

Alida looked into the faces around her. Almost everyone was smiling.

They had hated living so far from their home, and they all had long lists of things that they missed. Her aunt Lily wasn't sure they should defy Dunraven's law by going home. But she agreed the berries here weren't as sweet as the ones in the woods near Ash Grove.

"Almost everyone seems happy to be going back," Alida said when her mother came to stand beside her. "Except Aunt Lily."

Her mother smiled. "My sister is opinionated, and she isn't the only one who thinks this might be dangerous. But it's time to go home. If we do, maybe one day the dragons and the unicorns will decide to go back too."

"I hope so," Alida said. "I saw unicorns from Lord Dunraven's tower once. They were beautiful."

Her mother smiled again. "It makes me very glad to know that. I was afraid they were all gone from the forests forever."

"I wonder where the dragons are," Alida said.

"Don't worry," her mother told her. "They're hiding somewhere, too. They have to be."

Alida watched her mother walk back down the line, stopping to answer questions, bending low when a little blue-winged boy tugged at her sleeve. She wasn't dressed in a fancy gown this morning; she didn't look like a faerie queen. She looked like someone on her way to work in a garden.

Alida spotted her father at the end of the long line.

He had helped the weavers make magically strong harnesses for their goats. The wheelwrights had made stout little carts for them to pull.

Those carts were all lined up now, loaded with everything the faeries would need. Two of them were stacked with cheese and all the food from their root cellars. They had taken apart all their graceful wooden tables and packed them with care too.

Everyone's clothing—made of almost weightless faerie silk—had fit in easily.

Their big wooden plates and cups were heavy, though, so they were in strong willow baskets tied to the sides of the carts.

They had packed their precious glass jam jars too.

Alida remembered them from when she was little.

They had only thirty of them, a gift from a human farmer's wife long ago.

Alida fidgeted, watching her sister peer into one of the carts, checking her harp.

All the faerie instruments had been wrapped in soft quilts, then packed very carefully.

Alida wished they could play music as they traveled.

It had always lifted everyone's heart.

But she knew it wouldn't be safe.

Someone might hear the music—and they had to stay hidden.

Alida's mother had explained it to everyone the night before.

If Lord Dunraven was looking for them, he would almost certainly expect them to go deeper into the woods to hide.

He might think they would go as far as Lord Ermaedith's lands or even farther.

The *last* place he would expect them to go was the meadow he knew about—the one faeries had lived in for thousands of years.

That meadow was barely a two-day walk from the village of Ash Grove.

And Ash Grove was only a three day journey from Dunraven's castle.

Thinking about it like that made Alida feel cold and shaky.

Then she heard her mother's voice, clear and strong.

"Parents will carry their babies," her mother was saying. "Anyone who needs help will get it. The elder faeries can take turns riding in the cart with benches. Our oldest children will be leading the milk cows. We have brought flasks of rainwater. Use it sparingly, and we might not have to drink from streams."

When she finished, there were many questions. Once she had answered them, she looked at Alida's father.

He stepped forward. "Anyone who needs anything can ask me. I will walk last in line, to make sure no one gets lost or left behind."

Alida saw everyone nodding, getting used to the idea that they would be *walking*.

They all could have flown, of course.

They could have carried everything through the air, including the elders and the babies—even the goats and cows. But Lord Dunraven and his guards were always prowling, watching the roads and the sky. So the faeries would use mostly the narrow, hidden paths the deer and the wolves used.

The cows and goats could graze along the way. The faeries would be able to pick wildflowers to eat and her mother had brought cheese for Gavin.

He had offered to walk ahead of them where they were most likely to see humans. Alida watched him. He was smiling, nodding at something someone had said. The faeries had been scared of him at first. Some of them had never seen a human. Now they understood why he was Alida's best friend.

His grandmother lived in Ash Grove with her oldest friend, Ruth Oakes. They were both kind and brave, and without them Alida might never have found her family.

"Are you all ready to begin our journey?" Alida's mother called out.

"Yes!" the faeries shouted.

Most of them, anyway.

Now that the time had come, the ones who weren't sure were grumbling. One of Alida's oldest uncles was frowning. But when Alida's mother began to walk, everyone followed.

Chapter

2

At first Alida's mother walked at a slow, steady pace, glancing back again and again.

Once everyone was moving steadily through the trees, Alida went to walk beside her.

"Are you all right?" her mother asked.

"I'm a little scared," Alida said. "Why would old Lord Dunraven make such a terrible law?"

Her mother shrugged. "Your aunt Clare always says he thought daydreaming about magic and storytelling wasted time that would be better spent working. But humans and faeries are alike when it comes to that. Without stories and a little magic, we aren't happy."

Alida nodded. "The day I walked through Ash

Grove, I tied my shawl tight over my wings. I was trying so hard to look like a human girl. At first I thought someone might ask if I needed help. But no one did. They all looked tired and angry."

"The human farmers always had to give part of their crops to the Dunravens," her mother said. "We used to see the big, creaking wagons carrying off barley, wheat, oats, field crops of every kind—even cheese and eggs—all to feed the castle guards. I'm sure it's even worse now."

Alida nodded. It probably was.

Lord Dunraven had hundreds of guards now.

She walked in silence for a while, thinking about old Lord Dunraven, and his sons and grandsons and great-grandsons.

It all seemed so unfair.

"Before the law," her mother said quietly, "Lord Dunraven's guards would ride through the forests sometimes. But there weren't many of them, and the faeries weren't afraid of them."

That was hard for Alida to imagine.

Everyone was afraid of the guards now.

"When I was your age," her mother said, "there were guards visiting us when a flight of dragons flew over. We all stood there, humans and faeries, amazed by how beautiful they were."

"Are they dangerous?" Alida asked.

Her mother glanced at her. "The guards? Not then. They are now."

Alida shook her head. "I meant the dragons."

"Very dangerous," her mother said. "But only if something bothers them or scares them."

"And the unicorns?" Alida asked.

Her mother smiled. "Unicorns are kind and shy. I have never understood why the Dunravens would hunt them."

"How many Lord Dunravens have there been?" Alida asked.

Her mother glanced at the carts before she answered. "Twenty or more? I don't know. Some were much better than others." She leaned close to kiss Alida on the forehead. "But there have been more than a thousand faerie queens. And I am coming to believe that you will be the next one. Just keep walking," she said. "I'll hurry."

Then she spread her wings and flew, very low, all the way to the end of the line, where Gavin was helping one of her aunts lift something into a cart while it rolled along. Alida's sister, Terra, was carrying a baby, and she was smiling. If she was scared, it didn't show.

Alida kept her pace the same, thinking about what her mother had said. It felt very odd to be the one leading the way. She kept glancing back at her parents, her family, all her relatives and friends. She was so grateful to be with them again. Gavin, his grandmother, Molly Hamilton, Ruth Oakes, and John the stableman who had been the one to take her to Lord Dunraven's castle—they had all helped to free her.

"Some of the elders are having a hard time keeping up," her mother said when she came back. "Your aunt Lily is complaining already."

Alida nodded to be polite, then she made sure no one was close. "I have a question," she said quietly.

Her mother looked at her. "Yes?"

"There's a man named John at Lord Dunraven's castle," Alida began. "He was old when he took me there, and he looked the same when he helped me escape. Can humans live that long?"

"No," Alida's mother said. "But John is not human."

"But he doesn't have wings, and he—"

"He gave up his wings," her mother said. "In order to stay at the castle, to make sure you were not hurt."

Alida stared at her mother. "He's a faerie?"

"Yes."

Alida was astonished. John looked like any human.

"He wished his wings away," her mother said. "And he wished himself taller. He's very good with

16

horses, so he found work in the castle stable. He did it for me. To keep an eye on you."

Alida didn't know what to say.

Her mother sighed. "John used big, dangerous magic to make himself look human. I don't think he could get his wings back now."

Alida couldn't imagine not having wings.

Her mother touched her cheek. "John is clever. Most of the castle positions are passed from father to son, and the Dunravens never set foot in the barn. So he is safe. He hires the stablemen, and he makes sure none stays long enough to wonder how old he is."

Alida's heart was heavy. When she looked up, her mother was watching her.

"Being the queen is not easy," she said.

The first day of traveling was a little disorganized.

The goats weren't used to pulling carts.

The older faeries complained about walking.

By midday, the goats and the cows had calmed. But the youngest faeries hadn't.

They kept forgetting to be quiet. The older faeries shushed them at first, as if Lord Dunraven's guards were behind every tree they passed. But as the day went on, they began to chat, to point out patches of wildflowers to one another.

Alida's mother didn't stop until it was nearly dark.

When she did, most of the faeries lifted their hands and made balls of faerie light so that they could see to unpack what they needed for supper and sleep.

Alida's mother sent her around the clearing at a run to remind them that light could give them away. The faeries looked startled, then apologetic.

Soon the meadow was dusky again, with just a few dim lights floating over the carts.

And as soon as the faeries had eaten the flowers they had gathered along the way, everyone got ready for sleep.

Alida's parents and two of her cousins passed out blankets. The faerie babies were settled for the night, and the lights went out one by one.

"I'm glad we aren't near any human towns or villages yet," Alida's mother said. "There's one we will have to tiptoe past farther on." She yawned, then she smiled at Alida. "Come with me for a moment."

They walked slowly. The air was cool and the moon was a crescent in the sky.

When her mother stopped, Alida started to ask her what they were doing. Before she could speak, her mother lifted her hands over her head.

Alida stared.

Her mother was whispering, her fingers moving, weaving themselves together like threads on a loom, then separating again.

And suddenly she disappeared.

Alida was amazed. She had never even *heard* of magic like this.

"It's something I learned to do on my own," her

mother said. Alida stared. Her mother was *gone*. It was like the air itself was talking.

After a heartbeat or two Alida heard her mother whispering again, and among the other words she heard her own name.

And suddenly she could see her mother again, except she looked different—silvery.

"Am I invisible now too?"

Her mother nodded. "That's why you can see me."

Alida looked down at her hands. They had the same odd, luminous color as her mother's.

"I have been working on this for a long time," her mother told her. "It's not perfect yet. But it's close. It's one of the reasons I think we can go home now."

Alida's mother spoke two odd words and the silvery color winked out. "Are we still invisible?" Alida asked her.

"No," her mother said.

And then she began to teach Alida the words she had whispered.

Chapter

3

The next day's travel was a little harder for the faeries.

The path was narrow and it curved around boulders.

As they walked, Alida's mother asked her questions. For the first time Alida explained exactly how she had set Gavin free.

"I am so proud of you," her mother said, "figuring out the magic on your own. When I was your age, I could do only very small magic, the kind we would trade for honey candy at the Ash Grove market."

Alida smiled. "I remember the shoemaker."

Her mother sighed. "Maybe one day we can go there again."

"Will we be all right?" Alida asked. "Will Lord Dunraven's guards—"

"I don't expect it to be easy, Alida," her mother interrupted gently. "But we must find a way to stay where we belong."

She looked so determined, so fierce, that Alida could only nod.

Her mother glanced at the carts.

Alida turned to look too. The younger faeries were trudging along quietly.

But two elders were arguing about whose turn it was to ride in the cart.

Alida's mother asked her to lead the way again and went to settle the disagreement.

The next morning the path narrowed and began to slope upward. By midmorning most of the elders were riding in the carts. By the time the sun was almost overhead, everyone's pace had slowed. By noon they were halfway up a high ridge, following a zigzagging path that was still so steep the goats had trouble pulling the carts.

All the faeries had to help. Even the eldest.

The strongest pushed the carts from behind. Others carried bags of cheese over their shoulders to lighten the load.

But even with all the help, the goats finally stopped, too tired to go on.

"We shouldn't have come this way," Alida heard her aunt Lily saying.

Several of Alida's cousins started talking all at once.

The voices rose.

One of the faerie girls got so angry that she started to walk off into the trees.

"Cinder!" Alida's mother said, just loudly enough for her to hear. "The last thing we need is to have to look for you!"

The girl stopped, blushing.

She walked to the end of the line, her head down.

For a moment all the arguments stopped.

Then Alida could hear voices, low, grumbling, coming from the elders again.

"Listen to me! Going up and over this ridge will save us two days, and keep us far from the paths that connect the villages," her mother shouted so loudly that it startled everyone.

Then she walked downhill, talking to everyone she passed. Alida heard her asking if anyone was hungry, who needed a drink of water.

As she made her way to the end of the line, she stopped and patted the goats and cows too, rubbing their foreheads.

Alida watched, amazed.

As her mother walked on, the grumbling got quieter, then stopped.

When she got to Alida's father and Gavin, she whispered something to them.

Alida saw them nod.

While her mother walked back up the line, her father and Gavin leaned over the last wagon, pulling out one of the boxes.

They carried it up the hill and stopped near her mother.

Everyone was watching them.

"Can you all hear me?" Alida's mother asked, raising her voice again.

Everyone nodded, some called out, then it was quiet again.

"Many of us need to rest," her mother said. "We might not make it over the ridge today."

There was a little chorus of sighing and groaning.

"But remember, it will save us two days to go this way," Alida's mother added. "And humans almost never come up here."

A few whispery discussions started, then stopped, when Alida's mother pointed at the box.

"I asked our best cooks to make honey-baked

lilies," she announced. "Find a shady place to sit. We will bring them to you."

Alida and Terra ran to help their father and Gavin.

Before long the faeries were smiling, enjoying the lilies. And when they finally started uphill again, there was no grumbling.

Everyone kept an eye on the elders, helping when someone needed help.

They made good progress.

By the time the sun was close to setting, they had gotten the last of the carts over the top of the ridge.

They hurried downward, hoping to get to the bottom before dark, but they couldn't.

So they slept on the sloping ground.

Alida's mother and father both made sure everyone was as comfortable as possible.

Then, once everyone else had gone to sleep, Alida's mother led her a little ways from the others, and they sat close together, whispering.

"Have you learned the words yet?" her mother asked.

Alida tried to recite the strange words her mother had taught her. It was very hard. She made lots of mistakes.

Her mother repeated the words three times. "Practice when you can," she said, then kissed Alida good night.

Alida arranged her blankets and got settled down, then lay awake thinking.

She knew it was good for her to learn the magic her mother had worked on for so long.

The faeries might need it.

But she wasn't like all the other faerie children.

She hadn't grown up learning small, simple magic like they had. She wasn't used to it.

And this magic wasn't small or simple.

It scared her to be trusted with it.

* * *

In the morning everyone was grumpy, at least a little—no one had slept well.

Alida looked at Gavin. He closed his eyes and pretended to be sleeping, standing up.

She had to cover her mouth to keep from laughing out loud.

"I felt like I was going to roll down the hill all night long," Aunt Lily complained.

"So did I," Alida agreed.

Her aunt turned to look at her.

Alida smiled. "And I kept thinking that if I did, at least I would be the first one to make it to the bottom."

Aunt Lily didn't laugh, but a few of Alida's cousins did.

They started making jokes.

When Alida turned to shake out her blanket and fold it, she saw her mother watching her.

Chapter

4

The faeries kept walking.

Once, they heard hoofbeats, and about half of them leapt into flight.

They hovered in wobbly circles, shouting at one another to get out of the way, then realized it was only a herd of deer, startled by the wagons.

The faeries glided back to earth, looking embarrassed.

Alida's mother was shaking her head. She waited for everyone to quiet down before she spoke.

"If we ever do have to fly," she said, "the guards will have their swords and bows ready. If we do what all of you just did, flying won't save us."

Alida listened, along with everyone else, as her mother divided everyone into four groups.

If anything happened that forced them to flee, the first group would fly straight up, then angle a little way toward the west.

The second group would veer toward the east.

The third group would fly northward, and the fourth group would go south, just a little.

Once they were all up in the air, she would lead the way.

They practiced a few times, staying low.

Then they went on.

Alida could tell that everyone felt a little less afraid, knowing what to do if they had to fly.

A few times every day Alida walked off to the side far enough so that she could practice the words her mother wanted her to learn, without anyone noticing.

Then her mother showed her the finger-weaving movements, and the new magic seemed impossible to learn.

The finger-weaving was incredibly complicated. The words were long and strange and had an intricate rhythm.

Alida couldn't imagine ever being able to do both at the same time.

As they walked on, she practiced whenever she could. And she watched her mother walking up and down the line trying to think of things that needed fixing *before* something went wrong.

It made Alida wonder about the Dunraven family.

Their guards scared *everyone*: people, faeries, dragons, unicorns.

Had any of them ever been like her mother? Did they ever think about anyone besides themselves?

Two days later Alida's mother told her they were getting close to the village they would have to tiptoe past. That afternoon she asked Alida and Gavin to walk ahead and find a clearing hidden from the path.

Alida was glad to have a chance to spend time with Gavin.

In low voices, watchful and wary, they talked about everything as they walked through the quiet woods.

Alida convinced him to try dewberry blossoms.

He liked them!

Late that afternoon they found a meadow just off the road, hidden by big trees.

While everyone was settling in for the night, Alida's parents walked in circles, reminding the faeries to be very quiet and not to make faerie lights for any reason.

After the moon was up and everyone else was asleep, Alida still lay awake, listening to an owl, worrying. How would they manage to pass close to a human village without being noticed? It was going to be hard to quiet the elders and the babies and the goats and the cows all at once.

She was about to fall asleep when she heard her mother get up.

Alida listened carefully.

She heard the muted whir of faerie wings.

Was her mother going to look at the town? Alida knew her mother would be careful, but she was relieved when she finally heard the sound of her mother's wings again.

Alida slid from beneath her blankets and tiptoed away from the carts, following the sound.

"I tried not to wake anyone," her mother apologized as she came down, gliding until her feet touched the ground.

"Is everything all right?" Alida asked.

Her mother nodded. "I think so. But the village isn't as far away as I remembered, and two of the newer houses are close to the path."

Alida heard the worry in her voice. "How close?"

"We should travel as soon as we can, before the sun is up," her mother said. "I was hoping we wouldn't have to ask Gavin to go ahead of us, but I think we should."

Alida thought about Gavin walking past the houses.

He would have to hide, trying to make sure no one was awake or close enough to see the road.

Then he would have to run back. And if someone thought he was a thief, sneaking close in the dark . . .

She looked at her mother. "Let me go instead."

Her mother shook her head.

"What if someone sees him and thinks he's a thief?"

"He will be careful," her mother said.

"But what if there *are* humans awake, walking around?" Alida whispered. "Gavin will have to tip-toe away, then run to tell us. I can fly much faster than he can run."

Alida could tell her mother was thinking about it.

"I can hide high in a tree," Alida said. "I'll watch for a while, make sure no one is awake, then come back."

"You have to be very careful not to be seen," her mother said. "One glimpse of a faerie flying, and the story would spread. Lord Dunraven could figure out we're going home."

"No one will see me," Alida promised, trying to sound calm.

Her mother gripped her shoulders. "All right. Let's get everyone up."

And they did, explaining over and over why they had to leave so early, why everyone had to be quiet and hurry.

Alida woke Gavin and told him what she was going to do.

"Are you sure?" he asked.

Alida nodded.

"Please be careful."

"I will," she promised.

And while the faeries were getting ready to leave, her mother whispered the same three words in her ear and kissed her on the cheek.

Then Alida spread her wings and flew upward.

She kept going until she was above the trees.

The moon was up and bright, but it was still too dark to see the path clearly.

For a long moment Alida hovered. Then she turned in a circle, memorizing the shapes of the trees so she could find her way to the little clearing again.

The sky would soon begin to turn gray along the horizon.

She started downward, then stayed just above the treetops, flying fast.

The path got wider, and it curved around the biggest oaks.

Alida followed it, sliding through the rushing air, breathing in the scent of wind and dew.

She didn't slow down until she saw the first house.

It was painted white, shining in the moonlight. She perched high in a tree to listen.

At first there was no sound—no voices, no footsteps. There was a barn behind the house, and she

heard a horse fluttering out a long breath. Then, after a moment, she heard wood's mice rustling leaves.

Alida waited, listening to the silence.

She was about to fly farther, listen a little more, then hurry back to tell her family it was safe.

But then she heard hoofbeats.

It wasn't deer. It wasn't just a few horses in some human's pasture, either.

It was at least twenty horses, maybe more.

And as she rose into the air to go warn her family, she heard the faint clanking of metal against metal.

Lord Dunraven's men wore armor.

They carried swords.

Alida flew toward the rising sun, faster than she had ever flown before.

Chapter

5

Alida raced toward her family. They were lined up on the road, waiting for her. She was so out of breath when she reached them, she could manage to say only one word: "Guards!"

"Coming this way?" her mother asked.

Alida nodded, gasping in every breath.

"Do we have time to hide?"

Alida nodded again. "Hurry!"

Her mother whirled around and spoke quietly to the faeries at the front of the line. The instant she stepped away, Alida saw them explaining what her mother had said to the faeries behind them. They told the next family—and the message went down the line.

So within just a few heartbeats everyone had heard the warning.

"See to the goats and cows," Alida's mother ordered her, then she was whispering instructions to Terra and two of their cousins.

Terrified, Alida ran to make sure the goats and cows were led far enough from the road, tethered behind a copse of elm trees. Then she sprinted back.

Gavin was helping some of the elders around a crisscrossed pile of fallen limbs.

Alida started toward him, but her mother caught her arm. "Make sure everyone stands close together," she said.

And then she was gone, running to look down the road.

Alida got the elders gathered in one place, along with the faerie mothers who had babies.

"Make a circle around them," she whispered to everyone else. "Stand as close as you can."

No one questioned her. No one argued. Faster than seemed possible, everyone was in place and suddenly still, except for two crying babies. Their mothers soothed them quickly, and then it was quiet.

Alida could hear the hoofbeats. The guards were coming fast.

It would be all right, she told herself.

The goat carts and the cows were well hidden. The guards would gallop past and keep going.

Alida could see only a little strip of the road.

She spotted Gavin. He looked scared too, she thought. And only then did she realize it was getting light.

The sun was rising.

Her mother was keeping watch, hidden by the wide trunk of an old ash tree.

"Be still, everyone," she whispered. "And stay still. I don't have time to explain."

Alida watched as her mother lifted her hands, making the quick weaving pattern with her fingers.

Everyone was staring at her, silent, confused as she whispered the odd words, then recited the name of every single faerie. She did it so quickly that her whispering sounded more like wind than words.

Alida felt herself trembling. The hoofbeats were getting loud.

"You can see one another," Alida's mother said, "but the magic makes us invisible to the guards. They can still hear us, though. Don't talk, don't whisper, not a sound. Do you understand?"

Everyone nodded.

Alida glanced down at her hands. In the early daylight she could barely see the silver glow.

She glanced at Terra and her cousins.

They all looked scared. She was sure she did too.

As the hoofbeats got closer, Alida could hear the sound of clanking metal again.

Then she could hear voices.

The riders were arguing.

"HALT!"

It was an angry shout.

The other voices faded instantly.

The thunder of hoofbeats slowed, then stopped.

Alida felt her stomach tighten. Why would they stop here? Why weren't they just galloping past?

Alida looked at her mother.

She was standing straight and tall again. Her shoulders were squared, her chin was up, and she had one finger pressed against her lips. Alida understood. Silently her mother was telling them all to be brave, to stay quiet.

Alida couldn't see the horses, but she could hear them blowing out deep breaths.

They were fidgeting, jingling the buckles on their bridles.

The guards were talking in low grumbles again.

"Silence!" It was the same voice, loud and sure.

"We're falling asleep in our saddles, Commander," someone called out. "How much longer?"

"We will finish what we were ordered to do! DISMOUNT!" the commander shouted.

Alida heard the creak of saddle leather as the men all got off their horses and stretched.

The commander dismounted and stepped back from his own horse. Alida could see him through the tree leaves.

He was tall, and his face was as hard as stone.

Then he turned away. He was tightening the cinch on his saddle.

Alida held her breath.

It would be all right.

Tightening a cinch took a moment or two. No more than that. The guards would stretch and walk around a little, and then they would ride onward.

But then, behind the elm trees, one of the cows sidled.

A twig snapped beneath its hooves.

Everyone flinched.

The commander turned.

His head was tilted, and Alida knew he had heard the sound. He handed his reins to someone she couldn't see, and walked to the edge of the path.

Then he stood still.

Alida glanced at her mother, then at her father and Gavin.

The commander peered into the trees. "Is someone there?" he shouted.

His voice startled the goats, and they shifted in their harnesses.

"Come out here," the commander yelled.

No one moved.

Alida could hear her heart thudding.

She glanced at Gavin, but he was bent over, picking something up. A stone?

The commander was walking into the trees, squinting in the early light. "If I find you hiding, I will make you sorry," he said.

Alida could barely breathe.

The commander turned, looking over his shoulder,

and Alida knew he was about to call out to the guards.

She closed her eyes, stiff with fear. If they galloped into the woods, the faeries would be trampled. Maybe they should fly, all of them at once. Some would escape. . . .

"Sir!"

Alida's whole body jerked at the sound of Gavin's voice.

She opened her eyes and saw him gesturing frantically at her mother with one hand, pointing at himself with the other, waggling his fingers.

She nodded and lifted her hands, her lips moving.

Alida suddenly saw Gavin more clearly, without the silvery glow, and she knew it had worked.

He wasn't invisible now.

"Sir!" Gavin called out again, then ran alongside the path, staying hidden behind the long line of trees.

The commander turned. "Who's there? I command you to . . ."

Gavin lobbed the stone high, so that it struck the ground farther down the road.

The commander whirled toward the sound.

Gavin sprinted forward through the gap in the trees and slammed into him from behind.

They both fell to the ground.

The man leapt to his feet. He drew his sword, knees bent, ready to fight.

Alida could hear Gavin apologizing, his head bowed.

Alida exhaled silently when the commander lowered his sword.

"Explain yourself!"

"I stumbled, sir," Gavin said, getting up. "I heard the horses galloping and ran to see and—"

"What are you doing out here?" the officer demanded.

"Looking for a missing cow," Gavin said, his voice friendly, respectful. "Have you seen one, sir?" He walked a few steps farther so that he could see down the road. "Oh!" he said. "I've never seen guards before. I've heard about the silver armor on the horses and—"

"Have you seen anything unusual today?" the commander interrupted him.

Gavin walked farther away from the faeries, out into the middle of the path. The commander followed him, sword still drawn and ready.

"Up that way," Gavin said, pointing. "I saw a strange wolf last summer. It had a white spot on its side."

The guards burst into laughter, then fell silent when the commander glared at them.

Alida watched him frown at Gavin.

Then he pointed at the dirt, gesturing at the wheel ruts. "Did you see wagons or carts?"

Gavin nodded and looked surprised at the question. "Farmers come this way often enough, sir. And tinsmiths' carts. And sometimes the goatherds get down this far if the grass runs out before fall and—"

"Enough!" the commander interrupted him, sheathing his sword.

"Remount!" he shouted, and the guards' saddles creaked again. Their swords clicked inside their scabbards as they settled into their stirrups, then they all galloped away.

Gavin stood on the path until the sound of the hoofbeats faded into nothing. Then Alida saw his shoulders sink. She could tell how relieved he was— and how scared he had been.

Her mother wove her fingers in the air and said the two words that ended the magic. "Thank you for your wit and your courage," she called to Gavin.

Everyone cheered.

Alida smiled. She had been so afraid that her friendship with Gavin might cause trouble. Instead, he had saved them all.

"Do you think they were looking for us?" Alida asked her mother once everyone was busy getting the wagons back onto the road.

"I hope not," she said.

"But what if they were—"

"We can't stay here," her mother interrupted.

Alida nodded. She flew to the village once more.

This time a lot of people were awake.

She flew low and swift, looking until she found another path. It was narrow and bumpier, but safer because it was farther from the village.

Once they were a long way down the bumpy road, and everyone else had already thanked Gavin, Alida caught up with him.

He put his arm around her shoulders. She folded her wings tightly to keep them out of the way. "Please be careful once you get home," he said. "It'll be hard for you to stay hidden, even with your mother's new magic."

She knew he was right.

Chapter

6

After that the faeries traveled as fast as they could, staying off the paths and roads.

At first they were almost silent.

But it didn't last.

"I didn't know there could *be* new magic," Alida's cousins kept whispering.

A lot of the other faeries nodded, and most of them were frowning.

Alida's mother explained that the idea had come to her a long time ago, that she had been practicing it carefully. "We won't use it ever again, unless we absolutely have to," she promised.

"Good," an elder faerie named William said.

"That magic saved us, I know, but it's big magic. It *changes* something."

"I made it very carefully," Alida's mother said. "It fades in two days if I don't end it sooner."

William was still shaking his head. "Just be sure you don't teach it to anyone else."

Alida's mother didn't answer except to smile. Then she walked along the line to see if anyone needed help.

Two days later, when the sun was high, the faeries came to the meadow.

Their meadow.

Gavin caught up with Alida. "It's even more beautiful when we aren't soaked and shivering."

She nodded.

This was where their journey to find her family had begun—on a cold, stormy day.

"Wait here," Alida's mother said. Then she stretched her wings and flew in a fast, wide circle, skimming the treetops.

When she returned, she looked happy. "No sign of guards, and there are only a few new farms between here and Ash Grove, none too close," she said. "There are no new paths here or up on the ridge. I think we are safe for now."

The faeries danced in circles, celebrating for a few moments. Then they got to work.

The goats were unhitched. Kary and Trina, two of Terra's good friends, led them to the creek to drink and graze. The older boys who milked the cows every evening led them to deep green grass.

All the elder faeries were walking together, pointing, talking, remembering.

Alida helped Terra and one of the older boys unload two of the carts. Every time the elders walked past, she listened to what they were saying.

Nothing they had built remained.

Their wooden storage sheds had rotted into the soil. The pasture fence had fallen apart, and the log rails were mostly buried in leaves and dirt, brittle beetle houses now.

Every trace of their sleeping nests was gone too.

But there was a happy swell of voices when someone spotted a few of their blueberry bushes still alive.

And the egg-shaped stone was exactly as they all remembered it.

Alida helped unload a third cart, then looked around for her mother.

She was calling to two very young faeries who were flying around a tree, laughing.

Alida watched. When they landed, her mother scolded them.

Then she raised her voice. "Don't fly. Especially in the daytime. If we are seen walking, the humans won't be sure. But if we are seen flying, Dunraven's guards will come. Remind one another!"

She pivoted and walked away, heading for the biggest oak in the meadow.

Alida watched her mother stop beneath its

branches, and smiled. It was the tree she had recognized when she and Gavin had been here. When she was little, before she had been taken from her family, her whole family had slept high in its branches every single night.

Alida ran after her mother. Her father joined them. He looked up into the branches. "It's much bigger now."

Her mother nodded. "It looks strong, like it has a few hundred more years to live. Or more if we make sure it gets enough water in the driest summers."

Alida heard footsteps and turned to see her sister coming. "Our tree has grown!" Terra called.

"Do you remember it, Alida?" her father asked.

She pointed at the low limb that angled out from the trunk. "Terra practiced flying up and down from that branch," she said quietly.

Terra nodded. "Over and over and over."

Their father hugged them both.

Then they all stood silently, looking up. "Is this

still where you want us to sleep, Your Majesty?" he asked.

Alida's mother laughed and kissed his cheek. "Yes. Terra and I will find the blankets and sort out the rest of our things from the carts."

"Good," her father said. "Alida and I will get started on the nests."

Once her mother and Terra had walked away, Alida's father pointed toward the noisy creek. "First we need strong, tall grass."

Alida followed him as he walked the bank. "We want the longest stems we can find," he said.

Alida spotted a tall patch of grass on the other side of the stream. "There?"

Her father ran, spread his wings, and glided across, low and quick. Alida hesitated.

"Your mother is right," he called. "But that was jumping, not flying. And the water is cold as ice this time of year."

Alida ran, spread her wings, and glided across.

"Watch," he said, and showed her simple magic for cutting the tough grass. "See if you can do it."

Alida repeated the three words he had taught her and imagined a sharp farmer's scythe in her hands as she spoke.

The grass fell over sideways into a neat stack.

"You learn quickly!" her father said.

Alida felt herself blushing as they went to work cutting and stacking more of the strong-stemmed grass.

When they had enough, her father used magic to lift the first few piles of grass across the creek. Alida watched closely. She was pretty sure he was doing almost exactly what she had done to lift Gavin out of Dunraven's prison.

Her father looked up and smiled at her. "Try it."

Alida gathered the magic inside herself and moved it toward the grass and underneath it . . . then she gasped when the grass shot straight upward.

Her father helped her bring it down. "Use smaller magic," he said, "grass isn't heavy."

Alida found the magic inside herself again and kept it very small. She made it move more slowly, too, and once the pile of grass was on the other side of the creek, she set it down gently.

"You're like your mother," her father said. "You have a gift with magic."

Alida blushed again.

He touched her cheek. "We all missed you so much."

When they crossed the meadow, no one was flying. All the faeries were climbing the oak trees, their wings folded tight against their backs.

Alida's father showed her how to choose the best branches. She watched him bend the boughs gently, coaxing them into the shape of a deep, curving nest.

It was tricky.

By the time they were finished, she had learned a lot, including how to make the nest very hard to see from the ground.

"Now," her father said, "we need to find cattail stalks." They followed the creek and found enough for a thousand nests.

He showed her how to weave the green stalks into the oak branches. It was complicated. She helped hold them in place while he added new ones.

"We'll line it with grass," her father said when they were finished. "Then our blankets." He stretched. "This one will be big enough for all four of us tonight," he said. "You and Terra can make your own nest tomorrow."

"Does Terra know how?" Alida asked.

Her father nodded. "Better than I do. But if you have any trouble, I will help."

Alida smiled, then turned around, looking for Gavin.

It was easy to spot him, as always.

He and Kary were helping William, Aunt Clare, and some of the older faeries hide the carts, harnesses, and looms beneath branches and leaves, with a layer of weather magic laid upon them like a blanket on a bed so that rain and snow wouldn't ruin them.

When Alida walked up, Aunt Lily was telling everyone what to do.

She seemed happier than usual.

Alida suddenly wondered if her aunt had minded that *she* hadn't become queen. Or maybe she hadn't really wanted to?

"Did you finish your nest so that you can sleep like a bird?" Gavin asked, flapping his arms like wings.

Alida laughed. "You're just jealous because you can't fly."

"I am jealous," he said, and took her hand. "I am really going to miss you . . . and all this," he said, looking around the clearing. "But I need to go home to my grandmother and Ruth."

Alida knew he couldn't stay, but she didn't want him to leave.

He ruffled her hair. "They will both be worried," he said.

Alida forced a smile. "Tell them hello for me, please."

He looked up at the sky, then at Alida. "I'll come to visit."

Alida nodded. "Soon, I hope."

"I talked to your father about it," he said. "It can't be often, but I will. I just hope someday you can come visit us. Maybe for Winter Feast or after harvest. People sing and dance. It's fun."

Alida knew she should say something, but her voice was trapped inside her throat.

She could only nod and try not to cry.

They hugged. "Be careful, little sister," he whispered.

"Gavin is going home!" Kary announced.

Aunt Lily heard her. "The human boy is leaving," she shouted.

Alida almost laughed aloud, remembering how wary of Gavin they all had been at first.

Now they were all talking at once, gathering around him to say good-bye.

When he finally managed to leave, Alida watched until he disappeared into the forest.

Chapter

7

Alida and Terra had fun making their nest. The first night they slept in it, they lay awake talking about everything—including how brave their mother was.

"Would you mind being queen?" Terra asked her.

"It scares me to think about it," Alida admitted.

"Me too," Terra answered. "I don't think I could make decisions all the time. I'd be afraid I was wrong."

Alida nodded and sighed. "But one of us has to be queen."

Terra didn't answer, and they both stared up at the stars until they fell asleep.

* * *

A few mornings later their mother called everyone together.

"See that oak tree?" she asked, pointing toward the edge of the meadow.

Everyone turned to look. The oak was big, with a lot of low-hanging branches.

"If you hear hoofbeats or strangers' voices," she said, "tell everyone around you instantly. Make sure everyone knows."

She paused, her face serious and intent. "Then gather beneath that tree. Quickly. And stand close together."

Alida understood what she meant.

Everyone did.

Whether it was farmers from Ash Grove or guards or riders wearing silk jackets, her mother would make them invisible again.

It was a perfect plan.

The tree wasn't far, but there were no nests in it. It looked like part of the wild woods. There was nothing about it to draw the attention of the guards.

"Once we are invisible," her mother said, "we can simply be quiet until it's safe."

Everyone nodded.

"What about the cows and the goats?" a boy named Aldous asked. Alida barely knew him, but she had noticed that he talked to Terra as often as he could.

Alida's mother looked at him. "You can be the one to make sure they are tethered at the other end of the meadow, and use a little sleeping magic to keep them quiet."

Aldous nodded.

"We are going to practice at odd times," Alida's mother warned them. "Pretend it's real. It will be one day."

That evening when everyone was about to go to sleep, Alida's mother whispered, "I hear hoofbeats!"

Alida and Terra leapt up out of their newly made nest and glided to the ground.

The alarm spread fast, but the faeries bumped

into each other and it took far too long for everyone to get to the oak tree. They talked about how they could do it faster next time.

Then they went to bed.

Two days later Alida's mother interrupted dinner with another practice. They were faster. Much faster.

By the third time the families had made up ways to alert one another.

Some whistled like birds, others had hand signals.

Each elder was assigned two helpers. Mothers with more than three children got helpers too. The fourth practice was the best. No one hesitated. No one had to double back to find friends or to see if anyone needed help.

The fifth time Alida's mother whispered the warning everyone was gathered under the tree moments later.

Knowing what to do if guards came made everyone feel better.

Alida heard faeries laughing more, singing while they worked.

Her mother kept practicing the magic.

It was usually late in the evening, in the dusk, where no one else would see her.

Alida began practicing the magic again too, every night after Terra had fallen asleep. The words were getting easier, but her fingers were still clumsy.

She asked her mother for help and was almost sure she could do it once they had finished.

"Have you told anyone you are learning?" her mother asked.

Alida shook her head.

"Good," her mother said. "Keep it between us for now."

As her mother walked away, Alida wondered how many secrets she had to keep because she was queen.

The faeries worked hard as spring passed into summer.

They planted all the lilies they had brought with them.

They dug ditches to carry creek water to new flower beds and planted the wildflower seeds they had brought.

Alida took her turns watching the cows and the goats.

It was a difficult chore.

The goats would eat grass for a while. But when no one was looking, they ate tree leaves and chewed bark.

The cows were always trying to wander away.

"We need a fence, like we had before," Alida's father said one night as they were all eating their supper of flowers and berries.

"If we build fences, some human will think this meadow is a new farm and come to meet the new neighbors," her mother said.

Her father was shaking his head. "But we'll need sheds, too. We have to store cheese for next winter and the weavers need a place to keep the yarn they spin."

Aldous stood up. "We might have to keep using magic. We could make it so that rain, snow, and hail couldn't fall in a small area. Then we could make it so it never got too cold there either. And to keep the mice out—"

"A wooden shed is better for all those things than magic is," Aunt Lily interrupted.

"I wish we had caves here," Alida's mother sighed. "That's the only thing I miss about the other place."

"Could you make wooden fences and planked sheds that stayed invisible?" Alida asked.

"Maybe," her mother said. "But William is right. Complicated magic is always dangerous."

"I wonder why we came back here sometimes," William muttered. "All this hiding! It's all we think about now. Our queen is making *hiding* magic!"

"Before Lord Dunraven made his law," Aunt Lily said quietly, "we hired human carpenters to build a wooden bridge over the creek once. We paid them with good suppers and simple magic."

"I remember that old bridge," Alida's mother said. "I never knew who built it." There was so much sadness in her voice that no one said anything more.

Alida lay awake all night thinking. And just before dawn she got an idea. She slipped out of the nest and glided to the ground.

Her mother was walking around the clearing, eating dandelions for breakfast.

Alida ran to catch up. "We could grow small trees and tall bushes in wide circles around the sheds and the pastures," she said. "Blueberries and serviceberries and crab apples and wild mulberries, all planted in a jumble to look like they're part of the woods and—"

Alida's mother suddenly scooped her up and flew low in a zigzag pattern away from the nest-trees so that their giggles wouldn't wake anyone.

Then she glided downward. "Thank you so much,

Alida!" she said. "Simple and clever and no magic involved at all."

"You used to carry me like that when I was little," Alida whispered, breathless and laughing as her mother landed. "I had forgotten it."

Her mother nodded and set her down. "When you were a baby, you loved it." She looked around. "I just hope no one saw me break my own rule."

Alida meant to laugh. But all the sadness of the years she had been away from her family, all the laughter and love she had missed flooded her heart and she started to cry.

Her mother held her close. "I should never have let Lord Dunraven take you away."

"I know you had to," Alida said, wiping her eyes. "You're the queen. You couldn't think just about me. Or yourself. "

Her mother touched her hand. "I only hope you can forgive me. It was the hardest decision I have ever had to make."

Alida kissed her mother's cheek. "That scares me."

"The idea of being queen?" her mother whispered. "Making hard decisions?"

Alida nodded. "Terra and I talked about it. We're both scared."

Her mother held her closer. "You both have a lot of time to grow up and . . ."

She stopped midsentence and turned to face the woods.

Alida heard hoofbeats far away.

Without another word they ran in separate directions to wake everyone.

Before long the faeries were all under the oak tree, invisible. Alida was holding her breath, listening to the plodding hoofbeats, glad the cattle and the goats were tethered at the other end of the clearing.

She hoped desperately that it was lost travelers who would just ride past.

But the hoofbeats changed direction.

They came closer and closer . . . then stopped.

The faeries stood still as stone.

"This is it," Alida heard a man say very quietly. "A big, empty meadow."

Whoever he was talking to answered him in a whisper.

Then the first man rode forward, coming out of the dawn shadows and reining in so close to where the faeries stood that they could see him clearly in the gray dawn light.

A second man followed.

Both horses wore silver armor. The men carried swords.

Guards.

Alida pressed her fist against her mouth. Her knees were shaking.

For a moment the men just sat in silence. Then the second man shifted in his saddle. "How many times have you done this inspection, sir?" he whispered.

The first man glanced at him. "Once a year for

twenty-three years," he answered, almost too quietly for Alida to hear.

"Did you ever find anything?" the second man asked him. "Are the old stories true?"

The officer shrugged. And then he howled like a wolf. It was a high-pitched, jolting noise that startled the faeries into a terrified huddle.

Both horses reared. The guards reined them in tight circles to keep them from bolting. And then there was sudden silence.

The faeries trembled and held hands, but no one flew and no one made a sound.

"Are you . . . are you all right, sir?" the second man asked, his voice unsteady.

"Shhhh!" the officer hissed.

There was a long silence. Then he spoke. "The bedtime story in my family says faeries fly if they're startled and you can hear their wings. I didn't hear anything. Did you?"

"No, sir," the second man said.

"Then, they aren't here."

The second man laughed uneasily. "But the orders were to ride into every corner of the meadow once the sun was up. Then to search the—"

"I know," the officer cut him off. "I did all that at first. Now I don't. It's easier my way and just as accurate. If there ever were faeries here, they are gone for good." He yawned. "The yearly inspection is complete." He reined his horse around and rode back into the woods. The second man followed him, laughing quietly.

Alida held very still. She could feel Terra trembling beside her.

All the faeries were still as stone, listening to the clopping hoofbeats fade.

When the forest was silent again, the faeries glanced at one another, their faces full of hope.

If the guards wouldn't be back until next summer, they would be able to think and plan. They would have time to figure things out.

Chapter

8

As the day warmed up, the faeries ate their breakfast of flowers.

Almost everyone was happy and relieved.

Aunt Lily and William thought it might have been a trick.

No one else did.

"We can stand watch for a while," Alida's mother said, "just to be safe."

Everyone agreed to that, and she asked two boys to find a place in the trees where they could see without being seen.

Then the faeries began to discuss what to do next.

They needed sheds and fences, but it seemed

dangerous to build anything the guards would notice next year.

Alida's mother looked at her.

"I thought of something," Alida said quietly. She was nervous; everyone was watching her.

But her idea really was simple and it was easy to explain. And the instant she finished, a new discussion began.

The faeries had many opinions about what to plant and how to plant it. Alida's mother finally interrupted.

"We all agree on this much," she said. "We'll make two big, natural-looking circles. Once the bushes are tall enough to hide them, we will build a fence inside one and our storage sheds in the other."

"And a root cellar," William said.

Everyone nodded.

"The biggest circle should be on that side of the meadow," Aldous's father said. He pointed.

William shook his head. "No, that will cut us

off from the creek. We'll have to walk around it ten times a day."

By the next morning the faeries had everything decided and they were ready to work.

Tools were a problem.

They didn't have shovels, and they couldn't buy or borrow from their human neighbors anymore.

The strongest men ended up with the hardest chore. They used stout, sharpened sticks to loosen the dirt, and small, basic magic to lift it out of the planting holes.

Alida's mother gave all of the girls cloth sacks and told them to find baby berry bushes in the woods.

"Be careful," she reminded them. "Make sure no one sees you."

Alida showed Cinder and Terra and everyone else how to tie their shawls to hide their wings.

Then they all set off in different directions.

Alida's bag was almost full when she found a seedling mulberry tree. She used her stick to loosen

the soft soil. But the roots went much deeper than berry roots.

The sun was getting hot overhead. Alida turned in a circle. No one was near. She took off her shawl and draped it over a tree branch.

She dug deeper and deeper, using lifting magic to free the roots from the loose soil as she worked.

She was almost finished when she heard a sound.

She knelt and peeked through the trees.

All too close there was a human girl sitting in the grass, her back to Alida. She was making small, sad sounds, and Alida saw her shoulders shaking.

The girl was crying.

Alida sank to the ground, wriggling closer to the berry bushes, wishing she could help and knowing she didn't dare.

Then she remembered her shawl.

Without thinking, Alida whispered the words she had practiced, her fingers moving. But instead of saying names at the end, she breathed, *"Me and my shawl!"*

She peeked again.

Her hands and her shawl had the strange, dimmed, silvery shine the magic always caused—so it had worked. She was invisible.

When the girl finally stopped crying and left, walking slowly, Alida stood up.

She said the two words that ended the magic and tied the shawl over her wings.

She carried the berry bushes and the mulberry seedling home and smiled when Aldous got excited over the little tree.

But she didn't tell anyone what she had done.

She was embarrassed.

If she had been more careful, she would never have had to use the new magic.

With everyone working hard, by midmorning the next day the huge, crooked circles were planted.

The faeries had included five kinds of berries, all mixed together. Nothing was sown in a neat line.

All the plants looked as though wind and birds had scattered the seeds.

The day after that the faeries added lilacs, wild pears, briar roses, and a few gooseberries.

Late the next afternoon Gavin came to visit.

Everyone was so glad to see him.

Alida knew something was wrong.

"I am bringing you bad news," he said, "and I can't stay more than the time it takes to tell you. My grandmother made me promise."

He looked at Alida over the heads of all the others, then went on.

"There were guards in Ash Grove today," he said. "They came to tell us Lord Dunraven will claim half the farmers' crops this year. Not a third, as usual. *Half.* The big wagons will come on the first full moon of harvest. My grandmother and Ruth Oakes are afraid the poorest families will starve."

The faeries started to talk, and Gavin paused until everyone was quiet. "It took me a day and a half to get here, walking fast," he said. "But people will be gathering berries and hunting deer to feed their families. They could easily come this far. Ruth said to tell you to please be very careful and stay hidden."

There was a stunned silence as Gavin hugged Alida, then left, keeping his word to his grandmother. Alida ran after him with a ball of cheese, a cloth sack of berries, and a cup of water. He drank the water and handed her the cup back. Then he thanked her and hugged her hard, and went on. She watched him go, hoping he would be safe.

As Alida walked back into the meadow, the faeries were still talking. As she sat on the ground next to her sister, Terra leaned close. "I remember Ruth a little," she said. "Does she still live in that house out on the edge of Ash Grove?"

Alida nodded.

Terra smiled. "She must be quite old by now."

Alida nodded again. "But she's still strong."

"Taking more food means Dunraven is hiring more guards," William said loudly. "He has to feed them."

It made sense.

Alida felt her stomach tighten and looked at her mother. There was worry in her eyes.

Chapter

9

Everyone wanted to help the farmers in Ash Grove.

No one could figure out how to do it.

"In the old days we could have offered them some of the cheese we brought with us and a part of whatever we can make as the year goes on," Alida's father said.

"We can't give them anything," one of William's sons said. "Someone will wonder where it came from and someone else will whisper and . . ."

"We could give the food to Ruth Oakes," Terra said. "And she could—"

"No," Alida interrupted quietly. "We can't put her in danger."

Terra sighed and nodded.

The faeries began to argue.

Alida noticed that many of the ones who usually listened were speaking out.

Everyone was angry.

Would the guards come to Ash Grove more often? If they did, becoming good neighbors with the people of Ash Grove would be almost impossible.

Alida kept thinking about the girl in the woods.

Had she been sent out to pick berries?

Was she from a poor farm family? Maybe she had been crying because she was scared about her family starving.

As the summer went on, the faeries' meadow became more beautiful. The berry bushes and everything else they had planted grew so fast that Alida wondered if her mother had made more new magic. But she didn't ask.

Once the bushes and the slender trees were tall enough, the faeries built a log fence inside one of the wide circles.

It became a pasture for their cows and goats.

Inside the other circle they built three log sheds.

The biggest one was for the weavers. They would need room for their looms and spinning wheels, their spider boxes and bags of thistledown.

The smallest shed covered the entrance to a deep root cellar, where they would keep berry jam and dried lilac flowers and sweet winter squash and whatever else they raised in their gardens.

The third was for the cheesemakers to work in. As soon as it was finished, the faeries started saving every drop of soured milk.

No one said it aloud, but Alida knew they all wanted to have enough cheese to share and hoped they could find a way to do it.

"We need more glass jars," Aunt Lily said one evening when they were all watching fireflies. "We

are going to be swimming in berries. Too bad we can't go to Market Square."

Alida saw her mother sigh.

"We used to steal a handful of seed corn now and then on the way home," William said wistfully. "I miss corn. The cows would like it too."

Aunt Lily smiled. "We always left something in trade. Berries, or a good spoon carved from oak heartwood."

Alida's mother stood up suddenly. "We have to get used to the way things are now."

Her voice was high and angry, and everyone stopped talking when she walked away.

Alida followed her.

They crossed the meadow and found a place to sit in the soft summer grass.

"The longer faeries live in one place," her mother said, the words rushing out, "the more their magic seeps into the soil and the water. In the other place we had sick babies and elders every

91

winter. We tried to heal them all, but some died."

Alida stared at her. "Because there wasn't enough magic there?"

"Yes. I think being away from home weakened us," her mother said. "I haven't said it because I can't be sure. But when William and Lily talk like that . . ." She shook her head and looked up at the sky, then back at Alida. "It doesn't help. And I need everyone to help."

"Did old Lord Dunraven know about the magic in the ground and the water?" Alida asked.

Her mother shrugged. "If he did, he didn't care."

Alida remembered how desperate Gavin had been when he thought his grandmother might not get well without magic.

"When we lived here, did we help humans get well?" she asked her mother.

"Yes," her mother said. "But faeries also stole from humans sometimes. And no matter what Lily says, we didn't always leave a trade gift. Sometimes

we played tricks on people and sometimes they stole from us. But mostly we were good neighbors, until Dunraven's law made us afraid of each other."

Alida's mother stopped talking, and the silence of the deep woods settled around them. They sat close together and looked at the stars before they went to bed.

Alida made two decisions before she went to sleep.

She was going to do something— and she was going to keep it a secret.

Part of her reason for not telling anyone was that she wasn't sure she *could* do it. But even after she was almost certain she would be able to, she didn't talk about it. She was afraid her mother would think it was too dangerous.

And maybe it was.

But she wasn't like anyone else in her family.

She hadn't grown up among faeries.

She had spent so many years by herself in Lord Dunraven's tower.

None of the faeries had helped her. Not even her own family.

They'd had very good reasons for it, she knew, and they were sorry. But that didn't change the deep-rooted and thorn-sharp loneliness she had lived with for so long.

And it was Gavin who had saved her from it.

His love for his grandmother had made him brave enough to try to get faerie help.

No matter what the law said.

No matter how dangerous it was for him to try to free her.

Gavin was like an older brother to her.

Ruth and Molly had risked breaking Lord Dunraven's law for her too.

They would be doing everything they could to help the people of Ash Grove, she was sure. And so would she.

Alida did her work every day, but she practiced the new magic every chance she got.

She began flying over the village of Ash Grove while everyone was asleep. She memorized where the farms were, where the roads started and ended. Flying was much faster than walking. She could get home before sunrise if she hurried.

Her wings got stronger and stronger.

She flew higher and higher, too.

She found wind currents that pushed her faster than she had ever gone before.

Twice she circled above Ruth Oakes's house, thinking about landing lightly, figuring out which window was Gavin's, and waking him up to ask for advice.

But she didn't want him to help, just in case things went wrong.

Chapter

10

Summer was coming to an end.

The barley was turning from green to the color of good butter.

Farmers and their families were tying the ripe stalks into big bundles and stacking them high.

They piled the hay grass and began to cut the squash and pumpkins from their vines.

The winnowed wheat and millet were heaped up in mounds as big as the houses.

Twice Alida hid in trees in the daytime, watching, remembering what Gavin had said about harvesttime.

No one was singing this year.

No one looked happy.

The humans looked like the faeries did—scared, worried, and angry.

One evening Terra pulled Alida aside after a wonderful dinner of lilies, raspberries, and the most tender wood's roses she had ever tasted.

"I just wanted to tell you that I am grateful," she said.

Alida smiled. "Why? I didn't do any of the cooking or—"

"Not that," Terra interrupted. "I don't know where you're going at night or what you are doing. But I know it is something I wouldn't be brave enough to do."

Alida almost pretended that she didn't know what Terra was talking about.

Then she hugged her instead.

By the night before the first full moon of harvest, Alida was ready.

She knew where all of the haystacks and carefully

built piles of squash were on each of the thirty-six farms in Ash Grove. She knew where the farmers had stored their onions and piled their sheaves of barley, wheat, and oats. She knew the exact order in which she would visit each farm.

At the first one she used the lifting magic she had been practicing to move half the farm's harvest to a far corner of the field.

It took almost no time at all.

Then she wove her fingers in the air and used the names of the crops the way her mother had used the names of the faeries.

And it worked, just like it had with her shawl. In the moonlight she watched everything she had moved disappear.

She used simple lifting magic to make the visible piles rounded and neat again so that the guards wouldn't suspect anything.

Then she flew to the next farm.

And the next.

And then the next, getting farther and farther from home.

She was so quick and so silent that the farm dogs didn't even wake up.

But by the time she was almost finished, she was very tired.

She ran toward a huge pile of squash without seeing the human girl sitting beside it.

Alida stopped, scared, then realized the girl was asleep.

Alida recognized her. She was the one who had been crying in the woods. Alida tiptoed past. She moved everything but the squash and made it all invisible.

Then she decided she had to move at least some of the squash.

None of the other farms had piles this big now. The guards might wonder if the other farmers were hiding some of their harvest.

But if she woke the girl . . .

Silently, slowly, Alida moved almost half of the squash to the other end of the field.

When she was finished, she flew in a quick circle to see if she had forgotten anything.

Then she flew home.

Jittery, excited, and scared, she slid under her blankets. She couldn't sleep. She was hoping, with all her heart, that she had done the right thing.

The farmers would be furious when they woke up and saw half their harvest was missing.

They wouldn't suspect magic. No one in Ash Grove besides Gavin, his grandmother, and Ruth knew the faeries had come home. People might think some of Lord Dunraven's guards had robbed them. But no one would accuse the guards. They wouldn't dare.

By early evening the wagons and the guards would be on their way back to Lord Dunraven's castle.

The piles of food Alida had hidden would be safe.

As soon as it was dark, she would fly from farm to farm again, this time ending the magic.

So when the farmers and their families woke up, they would find a wonderful surprise.

Instead of less food for the winter, they would have more than usual.

Looking up at the stars, Alida imagined their faces.

Maybe they would dance and sing this year after all.

And they would figure out magic had been used.

They would figure out that their faerie neighbors had come home and were helping them.

Alida closed her eyes. It would be wonderful to stop hiding from the people of Ash Grove.

It would change everything.

Maybe she wouldn't have to hide her friendship with Gavin.

She closed her eyes and tried to sleep.

The next day passed slowly—too slowly.

Terra kept glancing at her, but she didn't say anything.

Alida helped pick the last of the berries, wishing she could go see what was happening in Ash Grove. That night she waited until everyone was asleep.

Then she slid out of her covers and glided to the ground.

She walked a ways before she flew, to keep anyone from hearing her wings.

And then she flew *fast*.

Chapter

11

Alida decided to go all the way to the girl's farm first. It was the farthest from the meadow. She would start there and work her way back toward home.

When she landed in the field, she raised her hands and began weaving her fingers.

"YOU! Stop that!"

The shout made Alida whirl around in time to see dark shapes rushing toward her.

She opened her wings to fly.

She was in the air, rising, when a strong hand grabbed her ankle. An instant later she was on the ground.

Alida struggled, but it was no use.

The people had a rope. Two women held her still while a man tied one end of it around her stomach.

It was too tight.

When the humans all stepped back, Alida saw three grown men holding on to the other end of the rope.

There were lanterns bobbing in the dark, coming closer.

"Don't touch her, her skin will burn you like fire!" someone yelled.

"That isn't true," Alida whispered, and managed to stand up. She was shaking.

The men holding the rope braced themselves, as though she were a wild horse that might drag them if she tried to escape.

"It *was* faeries," a woman was shouting. "You called my daughter a liar, but she was right!"

Alida tried not to cry. The girl must have awakened and watched her.

"I didn't steal anything," Alida shouted around

the lump of fear in her throat. "I just moved half of everything. It's down by the fence."

"Don't lie!" a woman yelled. "There's nothing but dirt down there."

"It's invisible," Alida told her. "To hide it from the guards. I can show you."

She raised her hands again, but a tall woman grabbed her wrists. "No tricks, you little thief."

Alida struggled, scared. "Just let me—"

"I've heard all the old stories," a man yelled. "No faerie ever did anything like that. She's lying!"

"Don't hurt her!"

The shout was clear and loud and close. Gavin was shoving his way through the crowd. Alida watched him, wiping the tears off her cheeks.

"Please let her explain, Mr. Dawer," Gavin said. "She's my friend."

There was a moment of complete silence, and Alida could see how shocked they all were at what Gavin had said.

Mr. Dawer was shaking his head. "She says the stolen food is still here, that she made it *invisible*. It would take a five-year-old to believe that. She's lying."

"No, sir," Gavin said. "She isn't. Bring the lanterns up here. Let her show you."

People grumbled and laughed, but the woman let go of Alida's hands, and five or six people with lanterns walked closer.

"Make me disappear," Gavin whispered. Alida wove the magic with trembling fingers and whispered his name—and he was gone.

"You can't see me," Gavin said. "Can you?"

Alida gave the humans time to gasp and glance at one another, then she made Gavin visible again. Before anyone realized she was still working magic, she made the farmer's harvest visible too—even though no one could see it in the dawn-dusk.

She pointed. "Everything is down in that corner of the field. You'll be able to see it now."

Mr. Dawer was pale faced, still staring at Gavin, but he nodded. "I'll go look," he said. "Sam? Bring your lantern."

The two men walked fast.

Alida held her breath and felt the rope tighten.

"It's all here," Mr. Dawer shouted up the hill. "Stacked neater than usual."

Everyone was staring at Alida. "I'm sorry," she told them. "I should have explained to someone, but I was afraid to."

"Let her go," Mr. Dawer said as he walked back into the lantern light.

"She might just fly off," one of the men holding the rope said.

Gavin stepped forward. "No she won't." He untied the rope and took Alida's hand.

People followed them from that farm to the next, and on from there. As the word spread through the town, the crowd got bigger. Over and over Alida wove her fingers in the air and whispered the words.

And every time, the farmers and their families thanked her before she left. Some of them had tears in their eyes.

"How did you know?" she whispered to Gavin as they walked.

"I heard the shouting and thought someone was hurt, so I ran to help . . . and saw you." He squeezed Alida's hand. "You are the bravest person I have ever known."

She shook her head, but she smiled.

When they got to the next-to-last farm, the sun was rising. People stared at Alida as the light got brighter.

Then, once she had made the last of the invisible crops visible again, the people who had followed her the whole way thanked her and started home.

When Gavin was the only one left, Alida smiled at him. "Maybe now we can visit each other more."

He hugged her. "I hope so. Do you want me to walk back with you, or . . ."

She shook her head. "I need to hurry. My parents will be worried."

Gavin nodded, kissed her forehead, then followed the others. Alida watched him walk away, then spread her wings and flew home.

When she landed in the meadow, all the faeries surrounded her, asking where she had been. Before she could answer, her mother arrived, guiding her toward their nest-tree, shooing everyone else back to work.

Once they were alone, Alida described every-thing. "So everyone in Ash Grove knows we are here," she finished, and let out a long breath. "I'm so sorry. I thought they would figure it out slowly, and have time to get used to the idea."

"You've proved to them that we can be very good neighbors," her mother said. "I think we should celebrate."

"They were so angry at first," Alida said.

Her mother nodded. "They were scared. Lord

Dunraven was taking a bigger share, then they discovered a faerie they thought was stealing even more . . . of course they were suspicious. And we have one more reason to be grateful to Gavin." She smiled. "Sleep while the rest of us cook. You can tell us the whole story at the feast this evening."

Alida climbed the tree and snuggled into her nest.

She closed her eyes, listening to the faeries arguing as her mother explained what had happened. When they stopped arguing and began to discuss who would make the berry soup and who would set up the feast tables, she drifted off to sleep.

When Alida's mother woke her, the sun was setting and the sweet scent of faerie food was in the air. "Come down when you're ready," she said, draping a pink, ruffled dress and a warm washcloth over the edge of the nest.

Alida cleaned up, slid into the dress, and tied the sash beneath her wings.

Then she hesitated.

If she climbed down through the branches and twigs, the dress would be ruined.

She jumped up and perched on the rim of the nest, intending to call to her mother to ask if she could fly down, just this once.

What she saw made her catch her breath.

Below her was a wide circle of dressed-up faeries, all hovering in midair.

Everyone was flying.

And when they saw her, they cheered.

"Just for tonight," her mother called out. "To celebrate your courage and our hope that the people of Ash Grove will be our neighbors again!"

Alida smiled.

She spread her wings and leapt into the air.

Follow Gavin and Alida in

The Faeries' Promise
#4: THE FULL MOON

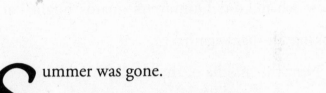

Summer was gone.

Nights were getting chilly.

One morning Alida could see her breath as she sat up in the nest she shared with her sister. Terra was already awake.

Alida stretched and tucked her wings under her shawl.

Then she followed Terra downward through the branches of the massive old oak tree. The edges of the leaves were turning brown.

The sun was barely up, but the meadow was already full of faeries.

No one was flying. They were all walking,

their wings hidden beneath cloaks and capes and shawls.

Every day Alida's mother made sure there were faeries perched high in the trees, watching the forest and listening for the sound of hoofbeats. No one knew when Lord Dunraven's guards might come looking for them again.

Near the middle of the meadow, Alida waved at her sister and Terra waved back.

Then they both hurried to begin their work. Today Alida would help weave sturdy floor mats from river grass.

There was a lot to do before winter closed in. The day before, she had helped her aunt Lily sort through all their blankets. Some had been torn on the journey home. Aunt Lily had taught her a simple mending magic. It had been hard at first, but Alida had practiced it until she could help repair the old blankets.

They would need many new blankets and

warmer clothes before winter came. The weavers were doing everything they could to get their looms up and working.

Most of the faeries were headed toward a wide, tangled circle of berry bushes and sapling trees. Any human coming into the meadow would think the bushes were part of the forest. That was exactly what the faeries wanted them to think.

But they weren't.

Alida had searched for seedlings in the woods and replanted them here, in huge, crooked circles.

A slender mulberry tree Alida had carried home was twice as tall already. The young blackberries, blueberries, wild pear trees, and woods' roses had all grown incredibly fast too.

Alida's mother said there was a thousand years worth of magic in the soil. Her sister Lily said it was even older than that.

Whatever it was, the uneven circle of trees and bushes was tall enough to hide the weavers'

and cheese makers' houses the faeries had built—
and their storage sheds.

They had planted a second circle of jumbled trees
and bushes at the other end of the meadow. That
one hid a pasture for their cows and goats.

Alida looked at the faeries around her. Almost
no one was talking. No one was smiling or singing.

The faerie flutes and harps were packed away. No
one dared to play music in the evenings now.

Everyone was worried. They were always ready
to run. Everyone knew exactly what to do.

If Lord Dunraven's guards came, the faeries
would race to the tall oak tree on the edge of the
clearing. They would stand close together so Alida's
mother could use her new magic to make them
invisible.

It had worked twice.

Both times, when the guards couldn't see anyone,
they had left.

Alida sighed. Her mother had taught her the

magic too, just in case. Every night before she went to sleep she recited the odd, ancient words. She practiced gathering her own magic and reciting the names of all the faeries, too.

Alida knew the guards would probably come again, sooner or later.

And when they did, it would be her fault. She was the one who had helped the humans. She was the one they had seen.

Walking to the creek to gather a stack of tall, strong grass, Alida made herself stop worrying long enough to concentrate on the new magic she was experimenting with. It wasn't big magic.

It was small magic—the safest kind.

First she used the usual cutting magic her father had taught her and watched a wide swath of the tough, wiry grass fall neatly on the ground.

Then she tried to mend it.

About half of the grass jerked upright and

balanced on its stems, but then it fell over again.

She tried a second time, then a third.

The fourth time, some of the grass repaired itself, the stems as strong as if she had never cut them at all. Alida smiled, gathered up the rest, and went back to the clearing.

All morning she helped two of her sister's friends and a few elder faeries weave mats for the floor of the weavers' house.

As usual, most of the elders acted like she wasn't there.

Kary and Cinder were nice, but Alida could tell they were a little uneasy around her too.

Everyone was.

Alida didn't blame them. It wasn't just because the villagers had seen her and knew the faeries had come home. She was *different*. She had grown up by herself, locked in a castle tower. Her best friend was a human boy and she missed him every day. That was very hard for the other faeries to understand.

Gavin and his grandmother lived in Ruth Oakes's cottage near Ash Grove. It wasn't that far away, but she couldn't go visit him. And he was afraid to visit her.

Lord Dunraven's great-grandfather had made the cruel law long ago. Friendship between faeries and humans was still forbidden. They were not allowed even to *talk* to each other.

Alida's family tried to obey the law. They had moved to a meadow far from this one, in a place where no humans lived. They had stayed there a long, long time until Alida's mother had realized the faeries couldn't be happy—or healthy— anywhere but here.

So they had come home, traveling at night, following hidden forest paths. Gavin had helped them move back.

Almost all the faeries had come to like him very much. But they were still afraid to have him come visit.

"Alida?"

She turned at the sound of her mother's voice.

"Have you seen your sister?"

"Terra's helping Aldous and his family," an elder faerie answered before Alida could.

"Thank you, William," Alida's mother called as she turned away, walking fast.

Today, like most days, she was dressed in plain clothes. She would work alongside everyone else.

If Lord Dunraven's guards ever rode into the meadow looking for the queen of the faeries, they wouldn't be able to tell which one she was.

Alida's mother was always busy. Every single argument, every problem, every decision, was her concern.

Almost every decision.

Alida lowered her head so no one could see the worry in her eyes.